Stone Arch Books
a Capstone Imprint

Benji Franklin: Kid Zillionaire
is published by Stone Arch Books,
a Capstone Imprint
1710 Roe Crest Drive
North Mankato, Minnesota 56003
www.capstonepub.com

Copyright © 2016 Capstone

Cataloging-in-Publication Data is available on
the Library of Congress website.
ISBN: 978-1-4965-0368-8 (library hardcover)
ISBN: 978-1-4965-2308-2 (eBook)

Summary: A wave of cyber crime using outer space
satellites has hit the world's biggest companies, and now
millions of dollars are missing! Normally this cosmic crime
would be no sweat for Kid-Zillionaire Benji Franklin and his
out-of-this-world problem solving skills, but there's
a problem: his parents won't let him miss any more
school! Can Benji ace his schoolwork AND save Earth
from the digital thieves?

Printed in China.
102016   010108R

BENJI FRANKLIN

KID ZILLIONAIRE

INVESTING WELL
(IN SUPERSONIC SPACESHIPS!)

written by
Raymond Bean

illustrated by
Matthew Vimislik

Table of Contents

Introduction

My name's Benji Franklin! After inventing a best-selling computer app that helps people come up with creative and time-saving excuses, I became the world's youngest and, well, only ZILLIONAIRE!

But I quickly discovered that life wasn't all about the Benjamins. I've decided to use my newfound wealth for the greater good—like saving the world from cloned killer dinosaurs, building super-powered rocket ships, and launching a solid gold submarine. Or two!

CHAPTER 1
Three Billion is Bonkers

Dad and I were out in the shop working on a robot he'd designed. It was a pretty cool idea, and he'd put a ton of time into it. As the robot moved, it created friction. The friction was used to create electricity, and the electricity was then used to continue powering the robot. You didn't have to plug it in or use batteries. It just went on its own. He'd built it out of parts from an old computer, a metal garbage can, and a pair of Rollerblades.

I was so focused on the robot that I hardly noticed the sound of a helicopter landing in the field behind the shop. I might not have even noticed it at all if it weren't for all the dust it kicked up. Dust swirled through the doorway like a sandstorm. I was glad I was wearing a welding mask

Dad and I walked out of the shop without a

word and looked at the copter coming to rest in the field. A year ago, I would have been shocked to see a helicopter landing on our property, but my life had become pretty exciting lately. I wasn't really that surprised.

The blades slowed and three men got out. One wore a fancy business suit and the other two wore all black. They all had on black sunglasses and looked like they were in the Secret Service or something.

The two guys stayed close to the other guy as he walked toward Dad and me. It was like a scene out of an action movie, but if it were an action movie, he would have walked in slow motion.

The blades on the copter had completely stopped by the time he reached us.

"I'm looking for Benji Franklin," he said, taking off his glasses.

"I had a feeling you'd say that," my dad said, pulling off his welding mask.

"I'm Benji Franklin," I said, leaving mine on.

"I can't believe you're really a kid," he said. He was pretty short, much shorter than Dad. He had a long white beard that didn't seem to match the fancy suit.

"I had a feeling you'd say that too," Dad said.

"Is there somewhere we can talk that's more private?" he asked.

I looked around. There wasn't another soul in

sight. The only other people were his two partners.

"Don't you trust your buddies over there?" I asked.

"I don't know who to trust these days," he said.

Dad waved for him to follow and walked back toward the workshop. The workshop and my house sit on property that has been in our family for generations. Most people would take one look at it and think it was a junkyard, but to me it was like buried treasure. Old car parts, pieces of boats and airplanes, and mysterious pieces of large equipment poked out from long, overgrown grass.

There were half-finished projects all over the workshop. Dad and I had been working, so it was even more of a mess than usual. I could tell Dad was trying to find something clean for the man to sit on but couldn't.

"I won't take too much of your time. My name is Mark Crow," the man said, clearly realizing there was nowhere for him to sit in his fancy suit. "I have a problem that I'd like solved as quietly as possible, and I'm told Benji might be the right person for the job."

I sat on one of the boxes a delivery guy had brought in earlier that morning. Mr. Crow sat on the one next to me. As I got comfortable, I realized I didn't know what was in the boxes, but they had been sent from my school. They were pretty big. It made me wonder what was inside.

"What's the problem?" I asked.

"Benji just finished a job," Dad said before Mr. Crow could reply. "He has a tremendous amount of schoolwork to complete, and I don't know that he'll have the time for anything outside of his studies."

I shook my head to indicate that I disagreed. Although I had just returned from a job, I was ready to get back to work.

"What's the problem?" I asked Mr. Crow again.

"It's kind of complicated," he said.

"Complicated is kind of my thing."

"I represent a very small but powerful group of business people," he explained. "Recently we've all been the victims of the same crime."

"What kind of crime?" I asked.

I was feeling more like a superhero than ever. I imagined my dad as my loyal sidekick. He's a little old for a sidekick, but what can you do?

"Benji is more of a scientist than a detective," Dad said.

"I've been known to dabble in a little detective work from time to time," I said, embracing my inner superhero.

"A robbery," he said, glancing over his shoulder.

"Where'd the robbery take place?" I asked. "Also, you do know there's no one out here watching us, right?"

"You can never be too safe. And to answer your question about the location of the robbery, that's the complicated part. It wasn't one robbery. It was many large robberies that happened all at once. They're probably taking place right now."

"I don't get it," Dad said.

"We own some of the largest companies in the world. We own fast food chains, clothing companies, sporting goods stores, credit card companies, car companies—you name it, and we probably own it," he said.

"Burger Slam?" I asked.

"We own it."

"Game Revolution?" I asked.

"We own that too, and most of the companies that make the games they sell."

"Jumbo's Food Mart?" I asked.

"Own it and most of the companies that supply the groceries for the stores. Like I said, if you've heard of it, one of us probably owns it. If you haven't heard of it, we probably own it. That's what makes what's happened so unbelievable."

"I still don't really understand," I said.

"Our digital transactions, when someone uses a credit card, are being hijacked."

"When you say hijacked . . . ?" Dad asked.

"I mean that the charges are going through—customers are paying by using their credit cards—

but the money doesn't go into our accounts. It disappears," said Mr. Crow.

"How much money did you lose?" I asked.

"So far, about three billion."

"You mean million?" I asked.

"No, you heard me correctly. We've lost about three billion dollars," he groaned.

If I had long hair, it would have blown back. "Billion with a 'b' like the word bonkers?" I asked.

"Billion with a 'b' like bananas," he said.

"WOW! That's, well . . . berserk!" I joked.

"No kidding. It's a bit of a nightmare to be honest. We're not sure what to do. We can't stop taking credit cards or our customers will think something is wrong."

"But something is wrong," I pointed out.

"Yes, but they can't know that. We have to conduct business as usual, but we're losing a ton of money in the process."

"You should really talk with the police or the FBI," Dad pointed out.

"We would like to keep this as quiet as possible. If we involve law enforcement, the story will be all over the news, and people might stop using our stores. We want this fixed quickly and quietly. We can't have people thinking our stores aren't safe to shop in."

"But they're not safe to shop in," I said.

"That's why I'm here talking to you. I need that fixed, and I need it fixed as quickly as possible."

"I'll have to talk with Benji's mother and his school about this before he can commit to helping you," Dad said.

"I completely understand, but we'll need to know in the next twenty-four hours. Every second that passes could be more money lost. Also, if news of this spreads, we'll have a major panic on our hands. So you can't tell anyone."

CHAPTER 2
Merci

"There's no way you can take on another job," Mom said that night at dinner.

"I know I've been super busy lately," I pleaded, "but this is an amazing mission."

"You mean 'job,' Benji. You get so caught up in them that they really become full-time jobs."

"Remember, he likes to think of himself as a superhero. So he prefers it if we call them missions," Dad said.

I nodded. He was right. I'd gone from being a kid that invented a successful app to a guy that secretly solved the world's problems. Why shouldn't they be called missions? Calling them jobs sounded so chore-like that it just didn't feel right.

"How about we call them adventures?" Dad suggested.

"It really doesn't matter what we call them," Mom said. "Benji needs to take a break for a while."

"Sir Robert thinks I should stop going to school for a while and focus on my missions and creating new apps," I explained.

Sir Robert had said it more than once, and I knew he'd mentioned it to Mom and Dad.

"Sir Robert is not your mother," said Mom.

"He is a billionaire who's traveled the world." I said, knowing I was pushing it with my mom.

"And as much as he's helped you, I'm beginning to wonder if he has your best interests in mind. But we're not talking about him right now. We're talking about you, and you need to experience a regular childhood and a regular education."

"But Benji has a rocket ship, a submarine, and more money than we can keep track of," Dad added.

"I think the whole 'regular childhood' thing might be a stretch at this point."

"I realize that," Mom said, "but I want him to have as regular a childhood as he can. I accept that you're already wildly successful at a very young age, but that doesn't mean you should stop learning and stop living like a regular kid."

"You always say to use my knowledge for the greater good, right?" I asked.

"Yes," she said.

"Well, this man that stopped by today said there are thousands of people who have been robbed. They need my help."

"That sounds like a job for the police."

"He wants it done quietly," Dad interrupted.

"Isn't there anyone else who can solve these problems? How come all these successful people are always coming to you to save the day?" Mom asked.

"You know the answer to that question," I said.

"A superhero, huh?" she asked giving a slight smile.

"I'm not like the rest of the kids, Mom."

"I realized that when you taught yourself French in kindergarten," she said.

"It does sound like an interesting opportunity," Dad added. Dad was funny. I could tell he was just as excited or even more than me, but he tried not to show it in front of Mom.

"If you can figure out a way to solve this," she paused, "mission, without missing any school, I'll give you my permission."

"*Merci*," I said.

"You're welcome," she said, giving me a smile. "School comes first."

"Agreed," I said.

Of course, I had no idea how I was going to solve the heist without missing any school. School was very demanding, and I'd missed a lot of it lately.

I knew I had a bunch of assignments piling up, but I didn't know what was due and when. I'd have to get my nose back in the books and get caught up if Mom was ever going to let me work on the mission.

I Get Your Point, But I Don't Like It

In the morning, my car picked me up earlier than usual. It was my first day back after my last mission, and I wanted to get on top of things.

"How was your last mission, sir?" Mr. Kensington, my driver, asked.

"It was a total adventure," I said. "I got to use my submarine, and I was attacked by a giant squid. It was pretty awesome."

"A giant squid! Wow! You're leading an exciting life these days," he said. "Were you paid well?"

"A few million dollars, and I'm part owner in a deep sea gold mine."

"Not bad for a week's work," Kensington said.

"Not bad at all!" I agreed.

He stopped in front of the school. "Let's hope your good luck holds up when you meet with your principal." I thanked him and walked into the school. I went straight to the principal's office.

She was on the phone, but hung up when she saw me coming. "Benji Franklin," she said, "how nice of you to stop by and say hello."

The tone of her voice sounded kind of like she was upset with me, which was strange because she was usually very cool.

"Is something wrong?" I asked.

"No, but you've missed more school than I had expected on your last adventure. I spoke with your mother about it, and we agree that you should take a break from missing school for a while."

"I know," I said. "We already talked about it at home." I realized there was no point in trying to get out of more school or make a pitch as to why I needed a few more days to work on the new mission. "I think you're probably right," I said.

"Good. You're going to need all of your attention on schoolwork in order to catch up on the assignments you've missed."

I figured I'd missed a few assignments, but it couldn't be too bad. She logged onto her computer and made a face. "Oh my. You have several assignments that are overdue."

"That can't be right. You said you were going to send me any assignments to complete while I was away. No one sent me anything to work on."

"I had asked Cindy to keep track of your assignments and pass them on to you since she's in all your classes," the principal explained.

"She didn't email me anything while I was away," I said. It figured too, because Cindy was always giving me a hard time about everything. She probably didn't send them on purpose just so I'd get in trouble.

"That's odd. Why don't you track her down and see if she'll catch you up on what you've missed."

OVERDUE
OVERDUE
OVERDUE
OVERDUE
OVERDUE
OVERDUE
OVERDUE
OVERDUE

I wasn't looking forward to seeing Cindy. She always gave me such a hard time about being out of school. She did help me a little bit with the mission, which was a nice surprise, but now it seemed like we were right back to her giving me a hard time.

I walked out of Mrs. Petty's office and down to my secret office in the storage closet. I held my hand up to the word *storage* on the door and it unlocked. I glanced over my shoulder to make sure no one was looking and slipped in.

I knew Cindy had been in my office while I was away, but I still couldn't figure out how she did it. The only way to get in was to scan your hand over the sign, and as far as I knew, I was the only one with the same fingerprints as me.

I sat at my desk and realized right away that my computer and all my screens were gone. An ancient-looking computer, like the ones in the classrooms, sat on the desk. I felt like I was in some kind of a time warp. I hadn't used a computer that old since I was a baby. The computer was probably older than me! I tried to log in, but it denied me access.

Just then I heard the door open and close. From behind the pile of boxes in front of my desk, Cindy appeared. "Welcome back," she said.

"How'd you get in here? Where's my computer?" I asked.

"Didn't your mother ever teach you to say hello to someone when they say hello to you?"

"Of course she did," I said, "but right now I would like to know where my computers went."

"Mrs. Petty gave me permission to remove them. We had them sent back to your house."

That must have been the boxes that were delivered the day before. "Why would she do that?"

"She realized, after I pointed it out, that it wasn't fair for you to have access to the latest technology when the rest of the students use the oldest computers known to humans."

"But she agreed to let me use this office," I said.

"That's true, and I tried to convince her that it was unfair and you should lose that privilege, but she said she had worked out some sort of agreement with you and that man Sir Robert."

She was right. Sir Robert had convinced Mrs. Petty that if my parents were going to make me continue to go to school like a regular kid, I should have a secret office where I could work on my missions in quiet. Mrs. Petty agreed. Now Cindy was trying to take that away.

"What do you care if I have a secret office?"

"Because it's not fair. I'm the head of the Committee for Fairness and Equality for our school, and I couldn't sit by while something like this was going on that is unfair for all the students."

"But how am I supposed to get anything done in here?" I asked. "These computers look like they came over on the Mayflower."

"Don't be ridiculous," she said. "There weren't computers when the Mayflower sailed."

I didn't have time to explain to Cindy that I was only kidding because the first bell rang.

"We'll have to find some time later today to talk about all the assignments you have due," she said.

"How come you didn't send me my assignments? I could have worked on them while I was away."

"I tried emailing you on the computers from school, but the connection is very unreliable. Most of the time the emails don't go through."

"Why didn't you just send it from your home computer or tell me when we talked on the phone?"

"Mrs. Petty asked me to email you the assignments from school. That's what I did. I tried from school several times, and the technology failed. That's not my fault," Cindy said.

I didn't want to spend another moment arguing with Cindy, so I slipped out into the hall and made my way to my first class.

As soon as I walked in the door, my math teacher handed me a folder full of work that was due by the end of the week. The same thing happened in reading, writing, social studies, and science.

I stopped into Mrs. Petty's office at the end of the day, plopped all the work on her desk, and fell into the chair. She looked at me and smiled. It was kind of weird, because I didn't feel like smiling at all, and she had a huge grin on her face.

"It looks like you have some work ahead of you this week," she said.

"I do, and I'll get it done," I explained. "But I don't understand why Cindy or my teachers couldn't have emailed everything I needed."

"The system isn't very reliable when it comes to emails and the Internet," said Mrs. Petty. "Cindy tried, but her emails must not have gone through."

"Don't you think that's kind of a problem?" I asked. "Everything takes place online these days. The school should really have better computers."

"You're right, but our system is very outddated."

"What about my office? How come Cindy snuck in and removed all of my technology?"

"Don't ask me how she got in. I don't even have access to that space, and I'm the principal. However, it did seem like the only fair thing to do. You can use the office,

33

of course, as we agreed. But I feel it's not fair to the other students if you're allowed access to better equipment."

"But those were my computers," I reminded her. "I paid for them. I wasn't using up any of the school's resources."

"True," Mrs. Petty agreed. "But unless you plan on buying new computers for the entire school, I'm afraid you'll have to use the same old computers as everyone else when you're in school."

I could buy new computers for everyone in the district if I wanted to, but it wasn't my job to supply computers for the district.

"As much as I'd like to help the school," I said, "It's not fair for me to buy them for everyone."

"Then you'll understand how it's not fair for you to have the best of the best while the rest of the kids have to work with the old computers."

I understood her point, but I still didn't like it.

CHAPTER 4
Name Your Price

That night, Mom, Dad, and I were at the farm checking up on the livestock when Mr. Crow landed his helicopter on one of the old runways. The farm had been an old airport before we converted it to a farm.

The same two Secret Service–looking guys from the other day were with him. He introduced himself to Mom and invited us all to go for a ride. He said he wanted to show us something that might help us make our decision. I didn't tell him that Mom had already decided to give me permission to take his mission.

"It's happened again," he said over the headphones once we were in the air.

"What's happened exactly?" Mom asked.

"The majority of all the money that exchanged hands today across the entire country for my group's businesses has vanished. One moment it was there and the next—POOF—it was all gone. We're talking about almost every transaction from our stores, websites, doctor's offices, and hospitals. It's a major situation, and we can't keep it quiet much longer. And when word gets out about this, we're all in big trouble. Worse, if our businesses suffer, the people that work in them might lose their jobs."

"Can't you simply track the money?" Dad asked.

"We're talking about electronic money, Mr. Franklin," Mr. Crow explained. "It's not like bills that we can put fingerprint powder on or track the numbers on the bills or something like that. This money is digital. It went somewhere in cyberspace, but we don't know where 'somewhere' is."

My phone vibrated. It was Sir Robert.

"Please do not breathe a word of this to anyone else," Mr. Crow warned.

"It's just Sir Robert. He's basically my partner," I said.

"No disrespect, but I don't want Robert knowing about what's happened," he said.

"You know Sir Robert?" I asked.

"Yes," Mr. Crow replied, "and I don't want him to know what's happened or that you're helping me. He's one of my competitors. I don't want him to have the satisfaction of knowing I'm being hacked. For all I know, it's him."

"Please put your phone away, Mr. Franklin," one of the guys in black said.

I clicked to ignore the call and felt kind of funny about it. Sir Robert had always been my mentor and someone I talked to about all of my missions. It would be strange working without his help.

"I realize that Sir Robert and you have a strong

history, but if you're to take this job, you mustn't breathe a word of the details to him. Do you think you can do that?"

I looked at Mom and Dad. "I can." I was really excited about the mission, but I didn't expect to have to hide it from Sir Robert.

I felt myself slip off into a bit of a daydream. There were so many things on my mind—the schoolwork I'd missed, the missing money, Sir Robert. It all swirled in my head.

"Do you have any ideas on how to figure out what's going on?" Mom asked. She knew me so well. Sometimes I slip into a bit of a haze, and then the idea comes to me. It's kind of like a waking dream.

"I do," I said. I had the beginnings of a plan forming.

"Your reputation for working fast is accurate," Mr. Crow said.

"It's not fully formed yet," I explained, "but I can see a solution to your problem. I think we can catch the hacker and get your businesses back to normal, but it's not going to be cheap."

This was always one of my favorite parts of the mission. It was interesting to see how people would react to the news that solving their problem might be fast but very expensive.

"If you can solve this problem, you can name your price," he said. That was the answer I'd been hoping for.

"Fantastic," I said. "Do you have any companies that sell computers?"

"Of course," Mr. Crow replied. "We own the three biggest computer companies in the country."

"I'm going to need a lot of computers," I said.

"How many?" he asked.

"About five hundred to start, but I'll need way more when the job is done."

"That doesn't seem like a problem," he said.

"I'll need you to deliver them to my school first thing tomorrow morning."

"I'll make the call the moment we're back on the ground," he said.

CHAPTER 5
Special Delivery

I woke up before the sun rose the next morning. I was super excited to get to work. I looked out my window and saw that the light in the shop was already on, so I got dressed and went down.

"What are you doing up already?" Dad asked.

"I guess I'm excited to get to work." I couldn't wait to see Mrs. Petty's face when those computers started rolling in. "What are you doing up so early?"

"I had a breakthrough on my robot last night. I haven't been to bed yet," Dad said. Dad sometimes got so caught up in his work that he worked through the night.

I felt my phone buzz in my pocket. It was Sir Robert calling. "I should answer this," I said.

"Hello, old boy," Sir Robert said. His face was

crowded in close to the screen on his phone.

"Hi, Sir Robert."

"How are you, Benji? I haven't heard from you since you returned from your last journey."

"I know," I said. "I've been busy getting back to my schoolwork. I have a pile to get to that's pretty massive."

"Tell your principal you're busy with things far more important than reports and homework. The world is your classroom now."

"Tell that to my mom," I said. "She doesn't even want me taking on any new missions."

"She wants you to be like other kids. I get that. I just don't feel school should be holding you back from your calling in life. Have you had any job offers since your last mission? Several of my business associates have asked for your contact information. Your services are very much in demand."

"Nothing too exciting. Like I said, Mom won't let

me take off any more time from school, so I can't do much." I felt bad about not telling him the truth, but I didn't know if I could completely trust him.

Later that day during second period, I noticed three massive black trucks roll up in front of the school. Through the window I watched as one of the drivers walked up the front path and went in the school. I waited for the announcement that I was sure was going to come over the PA system once Mrs. Petty learned what was in the trucks.

I looked at the clock. The announcement would come any second. I counted down in my mind. Five, four, three, two, one . . . It came right on cue: "Excuse the interruption. Would Benji Franklin report to the main office, please? Benji Franklin to the main office."

The kids in the class all looked at me like I was in trouble, but I just smiled. I couldn't wait to see the look on Mrs. Petty's face. I strolled out of class and made my way slowly to the office.

I walked in and Mrs. Petty said, "May I speak with you in my office, please, Mr. Franklin?"

"Of course," I said. The driver sat in the chair that kids sit in when they're in trouble and waiting for the principal.

We walked in, and she closed the door behind us.

"What's going on?" she asked once the door was completely closed.

"You said I could have my computers back if I

updated the computers for the school. I figured out a way to make that happen," I explained.

"Benji, as generous and considerate as that may be, you can't simply make a decision like this without asking me first."

"I thought we talked about it yesterday," I said.

"Well, I didn't expect you to go out and find a way to provide new computers to the entire school the next day," Mrs. Petty replied.

"Well, I did," I said. "It's kind of how I roll.

"It's not that simple, Benji," she said. "We are one school in a very large school district. I can't provide new computers to this school if the other schools don't have the same opportunities."

I knew she would say that and had already set it up with Mr. Crow so that I could get more computers if I needed them.

"If you allow me to install these computers today, I promise you that I'll get new computers for the entire school district when my mission is over," I said. Then I realized I was in a position to negotiate. "But I'd like something in return."

"I'm listening," she said.

"Give me a week off, but in the school. All my attention is going to have to be on my new mission. I can't be distracted by reports, late homework, and going to class. I also need you to forgive my missed assignments."

"This is highly irregular. Students don't generally come into the principal's office and negotiate their way out of missed assignments and going to class."

"But they also don't offer to supply new computers for the school district. I'm saving you millions and helping the school at the same time."

"You have a good point," she said. "I'll give you a week to complete your new mission. If at the end of the week you supply new computers for the entire district, I'll direct your teachers to forgive your assignments."

"You have yourself a deal," I said. "You also have new computers for the school."

"I've never experienced a student quite like you, Benji Franklin," said Mrs. Petty.

I wasn't sure if she meant that as a compliment or if she was criticizing me, but I had an opportunity to solve the heist, avoid my missing work, and keep my promise to Mom that I wouldn't miss any time from school.

"One more thing," I said.

"I'm afraid to ask," she said.

Then I said something that I thought might just knock her clear out of her chair. "I'd like to partner with Cindy on this mission."

CHAPTER 6
Invisible Data

Later that night, Dad and I decided we should head up into space. We needed to get a better look at the satellites orbiting the planet to have a better understanding of how they worked. We climbed into the cockpit, and my ship's computer said, "Good evening, Mr. Franklin and Mr. Franklin."

"Good evening, Saunders," I said.

Saunders opened the roof of the building. The stars shined about as bright as could be. We lifted off slow, rising up like a helicopter, hovering above the hangar. Once we were high enough and had cleared the building, I hit the booster rockets, and we were off like a bolt. Within minutes, we were out of Earth's atmosphere.

I turned on the GPS and asked Saunders to show us all the satellites in orbit. Then I asked Saunders to show me all the satellites owned by Mr. Crow's companies.

Saunders was a robot, I understood that, but I kind of thought of him as a person too. He seemed so human that it was hard to remember that he was simply a complex computer program.

"I'm displaying all the known satellites orbiting Earth in blue. I've highlighted the ones owned by the Crow Corporation and its companies in green."

"Thank you," I said.

"You do not have to thank me, sir," Saunders said.

"It's just a computer," Dad said.

"Yes, but he's extraordinarily smart." As I said the words, I felt something about the mission click into place. The transactions were done by computers. People slid their credit cards through the computers at the store and after that every other step was completed by a computer.

The reason why Mr. Crow and his companies couldn't figure out who was stealing their money was because the person stealing their money wasn't a person at all. It was probably a computer programmed to steal and then cover its tracks.

Luckily for me, I just had five hundred new computers installed at school. All I had to do now was program them to work together, and we might be able to catch the thief.

"Benji, are you okay?" Dad asked. "You haven't said anything in a while."

I had slipped off into a daydream. It felt like only a few seconds had passed. "I'm fine," I said. "Just thinking."

"We're approaching the first satellite," he said.

I looked out the window of the spaceship. The satellite was like a floating tube with mirrors and

long, flat panels on either side. The panels were solar panels and tilted toward the sun for power.

We zoomed ahead to the next satellite. It looked a lot like the first one, but it was much larger. The most interesting thing about seeing the satellites up close in space was that you couldn't see the data. It's completely invisible. Dad and I zipped from satellite to satellite. If you didn't know each one was transmitting loads of data back and forth to Earth, you'd think it was just a floating piece of metal.

There had to be a way to follow the data and track where it went and how it moved. For that, I realized, I'd need a few satellites of my own.

Dad and I had made and launched satellites ourselves in the past. We even have one that orbits Earth looking for dangerous asteroids. The ones we've made, though, were not nearly as advanced as what I needed for this mission. I needed a few satellites that could work faster than the satellites being robbed. And I needed them right away.

CHAPTER 7
Welcome To My Lair

That night I called Mr. Crow while we were in space and told him we'd need a few satellites immediately in order to solve the problem.

"Benji," Mr. Crow began, "I can honestly say that when I was put in touch with you I didn't really have high hopes that you'd be able to actually find a solution to my problem. I didn't think a child was capable of tackling something so enormous, but people told me to trust that you were capable of the task, and I did. Who knew there were twelve-year-olds with their own spaceships?"

"Actually, I'm the only one," I said.

"Of course you are," he said. "I will get you the satellites you need, but I'd also like to meet tomorrow morning to talk about your plan. Can you put together a price list for me so I have an idea of what I'm going to spend? I'll have to run it by my partners."

"I'll be at school tomorrow," I said. "But if you'd like to stop by, I'll be working on your mission. I'll send over exactly what I'll need and a price breakdown in a few minutes."

"I'll see you tomorrow then," said Mr. Crow. "Right now, I'm going to get to work on finding you those satellites. See you in the morning."

I typed out the bill for Mr. Crow and emailed it to him.

Fuel for spaceship	$175,000
Satellite delivery	$200,000
Total cost for project	$4,175,000
20% Consulting fee	$200,000
Total amount due	$4,375,000

*2,000 computers No charge, supplied by Mr. Crow (Value $2,200,000)
*Satellite supplied by Mr. Crow (Value $1,600,000)

The next morning, I had Kensington pick me up at four o'clock.

"You're really getting a lot of schoolwork done," he said. "I don't think I've ever seen you this committed to school."

"I made a deal with my mom and the principal. I agreed to not miss any school, and I agreed to solve the mission by the end of the week."

"It sounds like a lot of pressure," he said.

I guess it was, but I didn't think of it that way. To me it was an adventure and a game all rolled up into one. I'd managed to convince Mom to let me take the mission, and I'd convinced the principal to let me skip class all week. I had to succeed.

I was at school before Mrs. Petty. I put a note on her desk to call me when she arrived and went to my office to work.

I tried to hack my way into one of Mr. Crow's satellites, but it was too complex. Then I tried to access the computers at a few of his stores, but the code was too complicated to crack. I knew if I had more time I'd be able to get in without a problem, but we didn't have time. I'd have to figure something out—and fast.

Before I knew it, it was seven-thirty and my phone was ringing. It was Mrs. Petty. "Good morning, Benji," she said. "I just got in and saw your note. Also, there's a man named Mr. Crow and two other gentlemen here to meet with you."

"Super! Can you all come down to my office?"

A few minutes later they knocked on the door. I let them in and closed the door behind them. I had set up my computers already and was busy at work.

"What is this?" Mr. Crow asked.

"Good morning, Mr. Crow. This is my lair."

"I should have figured you'd have a lair," he said. "A secret hideout, stopping the bad guys—all you need is a cape and you're all set."

"You're not the first person to tell me that," I said. "I've been thinking about wearing a cape, but I think that might be going a little overboard."

"Just a little," Cindy said, walking in.

I didn't know how she'd made it in again! I'd closed the door behind Mrs. Petty and Mr. Crow. She had figured out a way to hack my security and instead of being mad about it, I was kind of curious.

"How do you do it?" I asked.

"I told you," replied Cindy, "you're not the only genius in our school."

CHAPTER 8
It's All About You

Cindy looked like she woke up on the wrong side of the cage or something. I decided it was probably the wrong time to ask her more questions about how she was getting through my security.

"I know that you and I haven't exactly gotten along in the past," I said.

"You can say that," she said.

"But I have a new mission, and I think you can be a big help."

"Why would you want my help?" Cindy asked.

"Well," I began, "you're always giving me a hard time about missing school when I'm on my missions. I thought that if you helped me with one, you might understand how important they are and get off my back."

"So it's all about you? Why am I not surprised?"

"Actually," Mrs. Petty said. "Benji's missions are usually about helping other people. If they weren't, I would never let him miss school. In this case, the people he's helping are the students of our school."

"Can I tell her what's going on?" I asked Mr. Crow.

"If you think she needs to know," he said.

I explained to Cindy that Mr. Crow's companies were being robbed and that I had a plan to stop it, but I needed her help.

"Why do you need my help?" she asked.

"You're the head of every committee in this school. You're used to working with large groups of people to get something done.

"I still don't understand why you need my help," she said.

"I'm launching a few satellites today that are going to capture all the digital activity at Mr. Crow's businesses. I've written a program that captures the data and slows it down, but the program is too long and complicated for me to enter it on my own. I don't have time to enter the computer code by the end of the week. Also, I think that whoever is doing the hacking on Mr. Crow's system has coded the computers so other computers can't detect what's going on. To catch this cyber criminal we're going to need eyes on the data, not just computers. This project is going to take the whole school. We'll need every student working."

Mrs. Petty leaned back in her chair and made a strange face, like she was in pain. I thought she must make the same face when she's in the dentist's chair.

"You can guarantee new computers for the entire district?" she asked.

"Guaranteed," I said, looking at Mr. Crow. He nodded.

"I'll have to meet with the teaching staff and see if they agree to this," said Mrs. Petty.

"Think of it as a team-building exercise. If we can work together as a team, we can learn so many skills we'll need in the real world," Cindy said.

"We never discussed this," Mrs. Petty said. "The school gives the student assignments, Benji. It's generally not the other way around."

Mrs. Petty was quiet for a few minutes, and then she said, "What do you think, Cindy? Can you put together a committee to write the computer code for Mr. Crow?"

"I can. And I will under one condition," she said. "I don't take orders from you. I'm in charge of the kids."

"This is all highly unusual," Mr. Crow said. "My partners are never going to believe I'm letting a bunch of school kids solve a multibillion dollar cyber heist. I'll give you until the end of the week, Benji."

"Are you in?" I asked Cindy.

"I'm in," she replied. "Let's get to work."

***

Mrs. Petty called a meeting with all the teachers to explain that for the next few days the kids in the school would be working on a school-wide computer project.

Cindy got to work breaking up my code into assignments for small groups. Each group would be assigned a part of the code to enter in the computer.

At nine o'clock, Mrs. Petty announced that we were having an assembly. The entire school stopped working and went to the auditorium. Cindy and I joined Mrs. Petty on the stage.

"Good morning, students," she said. "I've called you together to share some very exciting news. As you all know by now, Benji Franklin is often out of school because he has been working on top-secret missions. This week, you will all get a chance to be involved in one."

The room was quiet. The kids didn't seem to know what was going on. Mrs. Petty waved me over to the microphone. I'd never talked to a large group like that before and felt really nervous all of the sudden. I leaned in to the microphone, which I could hardly reach.

"Good morning. I know a lot of you secretly hate that I get to miss school a lot because of my super-cool missions, but this week you guys get a chance to be a part of one." The room was still quiet, and I couldn't tell what the kids were thinking. I knew I had to turn up the interest level if I was going to win them over. "Mrs. Petty has agreed to cancel classes and homework for the rest of the week!" I announced.

The room erupted. Kids acted as if they'd won the lottery or something.

Mrs. Petty made her way back to the microphone, and the room quieted. "We're going to work together on a school-wide computer-programming project," she explained. "While we're working on the project, I have canceled classes and homework. Cindy Myers will divide the school into one hundred groups of ten. Each group will be responsible for entering a string of code that will be part of the larger code that will help Benji complete his mission."

The room cheered again, and then Cindy took the microphone. "I'll email every student his or her group and the string of code to enter. Benji and I will be around if you need any help. We have only a few days to do this, so please work together and do your best. If we can complete the project successfully, we can earn computers for the whole school district."

CHAPTER 9
Invisible Money

The next day, Mr. Crow sent me the access codes and passwords to all of his satellites. Cindy and I helped each group at school to start working on writing code and linking everything into the new satellite. It was a massive job, but by breaking it into smaller pieces it didn't seem impossible. Cindy was really good about making the groups and keeping them on track.

After school, I was in my room waiting for Mr. Kensington to pick me up and drive me to the farm so Dad and I could launch the satellites. There was a knock at the door, and Mom walked in.

"Benji, I got emails from a few of the moms from your school today," Mom began. "When I told you that you had to stay in school if you wanted to work on the mission for Mr. Crow, I didn't expect you to shut down classes and put the entire school to work."

"I didn't either," I said. "But it's how things worked out. If we can pull it off, Mr. Crow will give new computers to the entire school district."

"I don't know how you do it," she said.

"I keep telling you," I said.

"Oh right," she said. "You're a superhero."

"I'm superhero-ish," I said.

I heard Mr. Kensington honk outside. "I've got to go. Dad and Mr. Crow are waiting for me at the farm. We're launching the satellites tonight."

"Remember, you have school in the morning. Don't stay up too late."

I grabbed my bag and ran out to the car. Kensington opened the door, and I jumped in.

Mr. Crow was waiting with Dad when I arrived. We all walked into the hangar. Dad had already attached the satellite to the spaceship. It looked a lot like the ones we'd seen up in space but was much smaller.

"It's all ready to go," Dad said.

"Well, what are we waiting for?" I asked. "Let's launch a satellite."

I piloted the ship up to the level of LEO satellites, lower Earth orbits. They travel at a height of about 100 to 1,200 miles above the planet. We released the first satellite and then descended to get the second.

After that we traveled a bit higher to the middle-level satellites and released the second one. Finally, we lifted the third satellite to the high-level orbiting satellites. Mr. Crow explained that the companies he represented controlled about two hundred of the satellites in orbit.

My plan was that all the existing satellites that Mr. Crow's group controlled would receive information like always, but the information would also go through my new satellites. The new satellites would work like a filter. My program slowed everything down and made it easier to understand what was happening and where things were going.

Each satellite's data was tagged with a code so we could track it as it moved through the system. One of the reasons Mr. Crow's company couldn't track the thief before was because of the speed of their system. It was always churning out data and didn't have the ability to slow down and look at where the data was going or where it was being controlled.

I remotely turned on the satellites from my ship and they blinked to life.

"Can you really keep track of all this data and make sense of it?" Dad asked.

"I guess we'll find out. It's amazing how much

money is flowing invisibly right now through all these satellites. There are billions of dollars just floating in the air. I'm not surprised someone found a way to steal some of it. It looks like the data is flowing through the new satellite well. The question now is whether the thief will strike again."

We orbited all the satellites a little longer to make sure everything was operating correctly, and then headed back to Earth. I felt like a hunter setting a trap. Now I just needed to wait and see if I caught anything.

CHAPTER 10
The Hero Never Sticks Around

The next day the kids at school had finished programming all the satellites and entering the codes. We spent the day monitoring and looking for anything strange, but nothing happened. All the money made by the companies flowed as it was supposed to from the stores, to the satellites, to the bank accounts.

I went home that day feeling discouraged. I had involved the school, I'd promised Mrs. Petty new computers for the whole district, and I'd promised Mr. Crow I'd catch the thief. The pressure was starting to really get to me by the middle of the next day. Kids were starting to look bored, and I could tell Mrs. Petty was nervous that the whole thing was a mistake. Then, on the third day, it happened.

All at once the money flowing from the stores to the satellites just vanished. It was like someone was doing an invisible magic trick—now you see it, now you don't.

"Benji, it's happening!" Mr. Crow said.

"I know," I said. "It's perfect."

"What do we do?"

"Nothing, for now just hold on and let the program do its magic. This is exactly what I wanted to have happen. My program is already slowing the data down and tracking the flow of the money. We'll know where it's going very soon."

The money kept disappearing. It would flow into the system of satellites and then disappear. As the data flowed in, the program slowed it down. Cindy broke it into chunks and sent it to the teams. The teams watched it in slow motion to see if the data flowed anywhere unexpected or if there was a gap in the flow.

At two forty-five, right before school was about to let out for the day, a girl in another sixth grade class shouted, "I've got it! I've got it!"

Cindy and I ran over. "What is it?" I asked.

"The satellite I'm tracking has a break in the code. A split second before the money goes into the bank a miniprogram appears for a fraction of a second and sends the money to another satellite."

"This is HUGE! All we have to do now is figure out who owns that satellite, and we've got our thief," I said.

I sat next to her and hopped on her computer. All the satellites orbiting the world are listed in a database. The database lists the registered owner of every satellite. I almost fell off the chair when my search returned the owner's name: Sir Robert!

"I knew he had something to do with this," Mr. Crow said.

"I'm sure you did, Mr. Crow," I heard Sir Robert say from behind us. We all turned in disbelief to see him standing in the doorway.

"Interesting timing," Mr. Crow said. "We were just about to call the police and have you arrested."

"By all means, call the police, but they won't be arresting me."

"Sir Robert," I said. "You own the satellite being used to steal money from Mr. Crow and his partners."

"You're right, Benji. I own the satellite, but I don't use it. I lease it to two associates of Mr. Crow.

Isn't that right?" he said turning his attention to Mr. Crow's assistants. The looks on their faces said it all.

"Why didn't you say something sooner?" I asked.

"I almost did, but then I learned that you were on the case and knew it would be only a matter of time until you caught these two." He handed me a computer disk. "This contains all the information you'll need to have these two locked up."

Things were getting messy. I decided it was time to call the police. We had the data, and we knew where the money was going. The only thing left to do was sort all this out and arrest the thieves. Within minutes of making the call, the police and the FBI arrived at the school. There were sirens and flashing lights everywhere.

"Mr. Crow looked devastated. "This is going to be huge news and terrible publicity for my group."

"It'll be big news, but I don't think it has to be all bad for your group," I said, noticing a long line of news vans streaming into the school parking lot. "When the reporters ask to talk with you, focus on the fact that you partnered with school kids to solve a complex computer problem. Talk about how the kids worked with satellites and programmed the computers to catch the theives. People will love the fact that you included kids."

"You'll have to join me to explain how you kids did it," he said.

"I'm not the one you want talking to the news people," I said, pointing to Cindy. "She is."

We explained to the police and gave them the data we'd collected. They arrested the two guys that had been stealing from Mr. Crow's companies.

Reporters gathered outside the school. Microphones stuck out in every direction. "I think we should go out and talk with them," I said.

We all went out, and they rushed over.

"Is it true your company was hacked and billions of dollars were stolen?" one reporter asked. Mr. Crow looked my way and winked. "Yes, that's true, but the thieves have been caught and the bigger story is our partnership with Principal Petty and the kids at her school," he said, waving Cindy and Mrs. Petty over.

It played out exactly how I'd expected. The reporters were more interested in the fact that a major computer company had partnered with a school to catch a hacker than the fact that the company had been robbed. Cindy explained to everyone how the school programmed and coded the satellites, and Mrs. Petty talked about how Mr. Crow's company agreed to donate computers to the entire school district.

I slipped around back and into the limo.

Sir Robert was already inside. "Benji, did you really think I was a thief?" he asked.

I felt pretty awful. Sir Robert was my mentor. I looked up to him in so many ways, but I had also doubted him. "I know it sounds crazy, but I did. I'm sorry. I should have known better."

"No need for an apology. If I were in your shoes I might have suspected me too."

"It looks like you've got quite the circus on your hands," Kensington said. "These reporters are going to want to talk with you too, you know."

"The hero never sticks around for a thank-you," I said. "Besides, I think I'm late for my cape fitting."

INVOICE NO: 1004968798

NOTICE OF PAYMENT

FROM: BENJI FRANKLIN
TO: MR. CROW

Fuel for spaceship	$175,000
Satellite delivery	$200,000
Total cost for project	$4,175,000
20% Consulting fee	$200,000
Total amount due	$4,375,000

PAID!

*2,000 computers No charge, supplied by Mr. Crow (Value $2,200,000)
*Satellite Supplied by Mr. Crow (Value $1,600,000)

PAYMENT DUE UPON RECEIPT

RAYMOND BEAN

Raymond Bean is the best-selling author of the Sweet Farts and School Is A Nightmare series. His books have ranked #1 in Children's Humor, Humorous Series, and Fantasy and Adventure categories. He writes for kids that claim they don't like reading.

Mr. Bean is a fourth grade teacher with fifteen years of classroom experience. He lives with his wife and two children in New York.

Glossary

access (AK-ses)—a way to enter, or an approach to a place

atmosphere (AT-muhss-fihr)—the mixture of gases that surrounds a planet

chauffer (SHOH-fur)—a person who is hired to drive a car for somebody else

hangar (HANG-ur)—a large building where aircraft are kept

remotely (ri-MOHT-lee)—from far away in space or time

satellite (SAT-uh-lite)—a spacecraft that is sent into orbit around the earth, moon, or another heavenly body